Influential Women

Marie Curie

Other titles in the *Influential Women* series include:

Influential Women

Marie Curie

John Allen

ReferencePoint
Press®

San Diego, CA

About the Author
John Allen is a writer who lives in Oklahoma City.

© 2016 ReferencePoint Press, Inc.
Printed in the United States

For more information, contact:
ReferencePoint Press, Inc.
PO Box 27779
San Diego, CA 92198
www.ReferencePointPress.com

LIBRARY OF CONGRESS CATALOGING-IN-PUBLICATION DATA

Names: Allen, John, 1957- author.
Title: Marie Curie / by John Allen.
Description: San Diego, CA : ReferencePoint Press, Inc., [2016] | Series: Influential women | Audience: Grades 9 to 12. | Includes bibliographical references and index.
Identifiers: LCCN 2015030321 | ISBN 9781601529541 (hardback) | ISBN 1601529546 (hardback)
Subjects: LCSH: Curie, Marie, 1867-1934--Juvenile literature. | Women physicists--Poland--Biography--Juvenile literature. | Women physicists--France--Biography--Juvenile literature. | Physicists--Poland--Biography--Juvenile literature. | Physicists--France--Biography--Juvenile literature. | Women chemists--Poland--Biography--Juvenile literature. | Women chemists--France--Biography--Juvenile literature. | Chemists--Poland--Biography--Juvenile literature. | Chemists--France--Biography--Juvenile literature.
Classification: LCC QD22.C8 A25 2016 | DDC 540.92--dc23 LC record available at http://lccn.loc.gov/2015030321

Contents

A Hazardous Collection

At the Bibliothèque Nationale (National Library) in Paris, France, there is a special collection devoted to the scientists Marie and Pierre Curie. The collection includes manuscripts, notebooks, and even personal items such as cookbooks and furniture. Marie Curie, who died in 1934, was one of the greatest scientists of the twentieth century and the first woman to win the Nobel Prize in Physics, an award she shared with her husband. Marie's notebooks are of great interest to historians and science writers. However, access to this material is limited. The notebooks are kept in lead-lined boxes. To handle them a visitor must sign a liability waiver and wear protective clothing. Marie's possessions still contain dangerous levels of radiation from her momentous experiments with radium and polonium, two elements that she and her husband discovered. That her personal items are still radioactive is no surprise. She handled vials of radioactive material on a daily basis, and radium has a half-life of 1,601 years—which is the amount of time required for radium atoms to lose half their energy. Marie's own writings attest to her blithe attitude toward the radioactive elements she was studying. "One of our joys was to go into our workroom at night," she wrote in her autobiography. "It was really a lovely sight and one always new to us. The glowing tubes looked like faint, fairy lights."[1]

Worldwide Renown

Marie's exposure to radioactive elements in her work led to the leukemia that ended her life. Yet hers was a life filled with remarkable success. Her discovery of the elements polonium and radium made her one of the first female scientists to achieve worldwide renown. In a field dominated by men, Marie demonstrated that a dedicated woman could achieve great things.

Marie Curie discovered the elements radium and polonium with her husband, Pierre. The couple was awarded the Nobel Prize in physics in 1903, making Marie the first woman to win the prestigious honor.

She was born Maria Sklodowska in Warsaw, which had been the capital of Poland before the country's division by war and treaty. Her schoolteacher parents instilled in her a love of learning and a patriotic feeling for Polish culture. She graduated high school with honors, but then developed a nervous illness that would affect her periodically for years afterward. She worked as a governess to help pay for college for her sister and herself. Moving to Paris, she earned degrees in math and physics at a distinguished university. While in Paris, she met Pierre Curie, a teaching scientist who became her husband and research partner. Together they performed groundbreaking studies on radiation and isolated new elements. Marie even coined the term *radioactivity*.

In 1903 the couple won the Nobel Prize for their work. Marie was the first woman to receive this honor. Three years later, however, Pierre was killed in an accident. Marie established the Radium Institute in his memory, and she used its laboratories to continue her probe into the mysteries of radioactivity. She won the Nobel Prize a second time in 1911. During World War I Marie and her daughter helped equip medical trucks with X-ray equipment to diagnose battlefield injuries. After the war Marie sailed to America to raise money for radium research. Until her death in 1934, Madame Curie—as she was called in press reports—reigned as the most celebrated and respected woman in science.

> *"We must have perseverance and above all, confidence in ourselves. We must believe that we are gifted for something and that this thing must be attained."*[2]
>
> —Marie Curie, Polish scientist and Nobel Prize winner.

An Inspiring Legacy

Marie Curie's study of radioactivity was crucial to science in the twentieth century. In addition to her discovery of radium and polonium, she discerned the atomic nature of radioactivity. This led to the harnessing of nuclear energy both as a weapon and as a power source. It also led to radiocarbon dating, a technique for finding the age of organic material by measuring the decay of the radiocarbon it contains. Marie and her husband studied how radiation can cause burns and destroy living cells but also has great medical value as a treatment for cancer and diseases of the skin. Today radioactive elements are used to sterilize instruments, irradiate foods to remove bacteria, and provide medical imaging.

Perhaps Marie's greatest legacy is the inspiring example she presents. She and Pierre demonstrated that great breakthroughs are possible with the proper dedication and dogged effort. Her achievement as the first scientist, male or female, to win two Nobel Prizes is impressive enough. But to have accomplished this in a field dominated by men was even more remarkable. Marie Curie remains an inspiration to young women who seek careers in the so-called STEM fields—science, technology, engineering, and math—in which they have historically been underrepresented. She proved that no barriers are insurmountable. "Life is not easy for any of us," Marie once said. "But what of it? We must have perseverance and above all, confidence in ourselves. We must believe that we are gifted for something and that this thing must be attained."[2]

Chapter One

The Floating University

In raising their children, two things were of supreme importance to Marie Curie's parents: hunger for learning and love for Polish nationalism. Both Sklodowskis were educators. Bronislava was headmistress at a small private school for girls. Her husband, Vladislav, was a scientist and physics teacher. The couple and their four children were living in an apartment behind Bronislava's school in Warsaw when she gave birth to Marie, nicknamed Manya, on November 7, 1867. Shortly thereafter, and not without regret, Bronislava resigned her post. The family moved to the site of a boys' high school, where Vladislav had obtained a well-paid job serving as assistant headmaster and teaching math and physics. The future seemed secure for this lively and intelligent couple, raising a family of future Polish patriots in their beloved city of Warsaw.

Politics and Polish Nationalism

The Sklodowskis' patriotic feelings for their native Poland soon landed them in trouble. In 1867 Poland did not exist as an independent country. In wars that took place almost a century before, Poland had been divided up among conquerors, including Austria, Prussia, and czarist Russia. Over the years, Polish rebels staged several uprisings—in one of which Marie's grandfather fought—but all of them failed. Despite a century of foreign rule, Polish patriots like Marie's parents nursed hopes that someday their country would regain its independence. For now, however, Poland was a memory, and Warsaw lay in the area ruled by Russia. Russian authorities banned any statements in favor of Polish nationalism, and Polish citizens were scrutinized for the slightest political misstep. Rebels were dealt with harshly. One of Marie's uncles had fled to France to escape punishment for his nationalist activities, while another was captured and sent to Siberia in Russia's frozen north.

Schools in Warsaw also operated under tight restrictions. Lessons had to be delivered in Russian, and mention of the Polish language or culture was forbidden. Polish could legally be taught only in private schools offering no diplomas. In public classes, students were expected to learn about the czar, Russian history, and Russian traditions. They had to choose their words carefully for fear of being branded as subversive Poles. As Marie wrote years later in her autobiography:

> The children knew that a single conversation in Polish, or an imprudent word, might seriously harm, not only themselves, but also their families. Amidst these hostilities, they lost all the joy of life, and precocious feelings of distrust and indignation weighed upon their childhood. On the other side, this abnormal situation resulted in exciting the patriotic feeling of Polish youths to the highest degree.[3]

Born in present-day Warsaw, Poland, in 1867, Marie Sklodowska (third from left), is pictured with her siblings: Sophia, Helena, Joseph, and Bronya.

In such an atmosphere, it was only a matter of time before Vladislav Sklodowski and his pro-Polish sentiments ran into difficulty. The Russian principal at the school accused Sklodowski of supporting Polish nationalism, slashed his salary, and eventually fired him. Sklodowski had to move the family to cheaper lodgings. His reputation as a troublemaker forced him to accept a series of lesser teaching positions. A failed investment swallowed the family savings. Finally, he and his wife resorted to boarding and tutoring young boys to make ends meet.

> *"The children knew that a single conversation in Polish, or an imprudent word, might seriously harm, not only themselves, but also their families."*[3]
>
> —Marie Curie.

Like her brother and three sisters, Marie did well in school. Her academic excellence began at home. She started to read at age four, and her father passed on to her and her siblings a love of Polish literature and culture. At school Marie was lucky to have certain teachers who skirted the rules and would read the class stories and fairy tales in their original Polish version. But Marie also endured hardship for her Polish sentiments. Once a visiting Russian official insisted that one of the students demonstrate her knowledge of Russian culture. Marie was chosen to recite the Lord's Prayer in Russian, which she did effortlessly—but also with the knowledge of how offensive such a recital would be to her parents. The official then demanded of Marie the entire list of Russia's czars and the names of all the members of the royal family. Again she complied, this time nearly in tears from the person's haughty insistence on Russian superiority. At last the official asked triumphantly who ruled over Poland. Marie paused but finally gave him the answer he was seeking: Alexander II, czar of all the Russias. After the official left, Marie fell into her teacher's arms and wept.

Two Family Tragedies

Not all tragedies in the Sklodowski household were related to Polish politics. When Marie was eight years old, her sisters Bronislava (named for their mother but usually called Bronya by the family) and Sophia caught typhus from one of their parents' young lodgers. Typhus, which

During Marie's childhood, Warsaw was ruled by Russian czar Alexander II (pictured), who expected his subjects to embrace the idea of Russian superiority and abandon Polish language and cultural traditions. Members of Marie's family, including her father, were punished for their Polish nationalist views.

typically results from the bite of infectious lice, causes fever and muscle aches. Bronya recovered, but fourteen-year-old Sophia died from the illness. Around this time, Marie's mother grew weaker from tuberculosis, an infectious disease of the lungs she had suffered from for years. Due to her condition, she had always taken care to limit her kisses and hugs with the children for fear of infecting them. Marie would retain memories of her mother stroking her head as a tender mark of affection. Marie's daughter Ève wrote years later, "Manya had an infinite love for her mother. It seemed to her that no other creature on earth could be so graceful, so good or so wise."[4] As Bronislava's condition worsened, she became thin and feverish and frequently coughed blood. On May 9, 1878, she died. She was only forty-two years old. Heartbroken, Marie grew depressed and had feelings of hopelessness. She despaired that all of her prayers and those of her family members had failed to save her mother. While Marie continued to attend church as before, she never again expressed belief in religion.

Bronislava's death brought the rest of the family even closer together. During the week, the children worked hard at school and looked forward to Saturday nights, when their father would read to them from classic Polish literature. He also introduced them to the scientific topics that he loved, particularly in physics. When Russian authorities ended the teaching of laboratory methods in Polish schools, Vladislav brought his classroom equipment home and used it to teach Marie and her siblings the basics of performing experiments. He instilled in his youngest daughter a passion for science and research that would last a lifetime.

School Success and Nervous Collapse

Marie threw herself into her schoolwork with a renewed energy. At home she read constantly, everything from poetry and adventure stories to her father's journals on physics. She also had a facility for languages. At age fifteen she graduated secondary school, receiving a gold medal as the top student in her class. The only thing that tainted her proud moment was being forced to shake the hand of the education minister, a pompous Russian.

After graduation Marie experienced a collapse that doctors blamed on nerves and exhaustion. It seems to have been a recurrence of the depression that would afflict her periodically throughout her life. Her father suggested a therapeutic visit to cousins in the south of Poland. Marie spent a year there enjoying a whirlwind of social gatherings and rural dance festivals called *kuligs*. In a letter to a friend, she described one of the dances: "There were a great many young men from

An Oppressed Country

The Poland that Marie Curie knew as a child was an occupied country, forced to live under Russian control. Polish patriots knew it was not always so. From the Middle Ages, when it was a powerful kingdom, to the 1700s, Poland had thrived. It once was the largest European country in size. It organized one of Europe's first legislatures and later enacted its first constitution. However, despite these political innovations, Poland lacked a strong central government. In the 1770s its aggressive neighbors, Russia, Prussia, and Austria, began to seize Polish territory for themselves. The German kingdom of Prussia took lands in the northwest (what is now northern Poland), while Russia occupied territory in the northeast (what is now Belarus), and Austria took Galicia in the southwest. In 1795 Poland's central territory was divided among its conquerors, and the Polish king abdicated. Poland vanished from maps of Europe.

In 1807 the French ruler and military commander Napoleon Bonaparte captured certain Polish territories and combined them into the Duchy of Warsaw under French control. But Napoleon's defeat in 1815 enabled Russia, Prussia, and Austria to reclaim their Polish lands. Europe's great powers relegated Poland to a semi-independent state ruled by Russia's czar. Patriotic Poles chafed at the situation, rising up in periodic rebellion in 1830, 1846, and 1863. Each revolt was put down more harshly than the last. By Marie's time, Poland existed under a strict Russian regime that suppressed Polish language, culture, and patriotic sentiment.

Cracow, very handsome boys who danced so well! . . . At eight o'clock in the morning we danced the last dance—a white mazurka."[5] She continued to study, but she also made time for exploring the woods and swimming in the river. She enjoyed staying in the homes of her uncles, which were filled with emblems of Polish culture, including music, art, books, and lively conversation. In the spring Marie's sister

Helena joined her in the south. They visited the luxurious country estate of one of their mother's former students. The sisters spent carefree days lolling in the sunshine and playing practical jokes. Marie always cherished the memory of her restful year in the country.

A Special Night School

Refreshed in spirit, Marie returned to Warsaw. There she found a household in greater turmoil than before. Her father's finances had not improved, and most of what money there was went to support Marie's brother, Joseph, in his medical studies at the University of Warsaw. What with financial worries and job pressures, her father's health was failing. Marie and her sister Bronya dreamed of following Joseph's path to a college education—Bronya wanted to become a physician herself—but at that time Polish universities did not admit women. Marie took jobs tutoring students to bring in some money. In her spare time she studied and confided to her journal how much she longed for intellectual stimulus.

> *"[The Floating University was] begun by Polish scholars in the late 1800s to create greater educational opportunities and to resist the suppression of their culture."[6]*
>
> —Historian Megan Abigail White.

To continue their education, Marie and Bronya decided to attend the so-called Floating University. This was an illegal night school whose name referred to the fact that the classes moved from place to place to avoid detection by czarist authorities. The Floating University was "begun by Polish scholars in the late 1800s to create greater educational opportunities and to resist the suppression of their culture," according to historian Megan Abigail White. "Meetings were small and were held in private homes and apartments."[6] The driving force behind the school was a woman named Jadwiga Szczasinska Dawidowa. She not only organized the original meetings but also took pride in outsmarting the Russian police. At the time Marie enrolled, Dawidowa's clandestine school system had more than one thousand students. The homes used for meetings belonged to families in Marie's social circle who shared the same patriotic fervor. Some of the hostesses had lost their husbands to exile or death at the hands of the authorities. Students drew inspiration from meeting these forceful and self-sufficient women who encouraged them in their studies. They believed their work at this secret academy was important for the future of Poland. Modest fees helped pay for books, although the fees were waived for poorer students. The Floating University offered courses in mathematics, anatomy, natural history, and the humanities. It also presented an opportunity to mix with other intelligent young women who shared Marie's zest for knowledge and patriotic attachment to Poland. The Floating University helped convince Marie to continue her pursuit of an education despite all the obstacles she faced, both financial and political.

Around this time Marie took a daytime job as a governess for a wealthy family of lawyers. Typically, a governess was hired to tutor the children of a prosperous family at home. Marie found her employers

Marie's brother, Joseph, studied medicine at the University of Warsaw (pictured). Because the university did not admit women, Marie and her sister Bronya attended the Floating University, an illegal night school that was moved from place to place to avoid detection by czarist authorities.

unbearable, their talk constantly filled with gossip and slander. Disillusioned with her job, she soon offered her sister Bronya a new plan. Bronya would attend medical school at the prestigious Sorbonne in Paris, using her own savings to pay for the first year. Subsequently, Marie would send monthly payments from her earnings as a governess until Bronya became a doctor. At that point Marie would follow her sister to Paris and pursue her own degree. The plan suited the sisters' joint ambitions perfectly. In October 1885 the whole family saw Bronya off at the train station. Afterward Marie swore to herself that she must find a better job.

Work and Romance in the Country

After some hesitation, Marie, now eighteen, accepted another job as a governess. This required her to move to the country, 50 miles (80 km) north of her beloved Warsaw. It was a momentous decision. "That going away," she wrote in her autobiography, "remains one of the most vivid memories of my youth. My heart was heavy as I climbed into the railway car. It was to carry me for several hours, away from those I loved."[7] At least the pay was good—five hundred rubles a year. Marie decided to make the best of it, hoping to find her new employers more likable.

> "That going away remains one of the most vivid memories of my youth. My heart was heavy as I climbed into the railway car."[7]
>
> —Marie Curie, in her autobiography.

She need not have worried. The Zorawskis welcomed her into their manor home like one of the family and treated her with great kindness. Juliusz Zorawski was the owner of a thriving sugar beet factory. The Zorawskis' two sons were away at school, and Marie's job was to educate two of their daughters. Bronka, the eldest girl, was Marie's age and soon became a friend. The younger girl, Andzia, lacked concentration and tended to be unruly. Marie worked hard to help her charges pass their examinations. At night she turned to her own studies, still dreaming of Paris and the university. In a letter to her cousin, she mentioned three books she was reading—one in English, one in French, and one in Russian. She also found time to give reading lessons to the illiterate children of

The January Uprising

The political event that had the greatest effect on the lives of Marie and her family occurred several years before she was born. The January Uprising began on January 22, 1863. It was a spontaneous protest by thousands of young Polish males against the Russian policy of *branka*. This was compulsory military service in the Russian army, often for terms as long as twenty-five years. Most Poles subject to this policy had been identified by Russian authorities as members of revolutionary groups. These patriots (a group that included nobles, intellectuals, and peasants) reacted by taking up arms to end the Russian occupation of their homeland.

Tactics on both sides were vicious. With no standing army, the Polish fighters had to resort to guerrilla warfare. They carried out assassinations of Russian officers and civilian leaders. They also targeted fellow Poles who helped the enemy. Russian commanders ordered their troops to take no prisoners. Villagers in the countryside risked death by aiding the insurgents. After a year and a half of fighting, Russian forces finally crushed the uprising. Czar Alexander II quickly took steps to discourage any future revolt. Rebels faced public execution or deportation to Siberia. Use of the Polish language or displays of Polish culture were outlawed. Russian became the official language. Polish schools and government agencies were replaced by Russian-led versions. For families like Marie's who yearned for an independent Poland, the failure of the January Uprising ushered in a bleak period of Russian tyranny.

Zorawski's peasant workers. Marie saw that her employer shared her father's patriotic zeal when he approved of her work on the side. Had the Russian authorities found out about the lessons, Zorawski might have been jailed or shipped to Siberia for treasonous activity.

Marie's life with the Zorawskis took an unexpected turn when she met the eldest son, Kazimierz. Handsome and brilliant, Kazimierz was studying mathematics at the University of Warsaw. He was immediately taken with this young governess, with her wit and intelligence, her manners and dancing skill, and her love of sports like skating and boating. Marie did not defer to his opinions but staunchly defended her own ideas. Kazimierz's visits home grew more frequent. Soon the couple began to discuss marriage. However, when Kazimierz's parents learned of their plans, they were outraged. They were fond of Marie, but her position as a penniless governess could not be ignored. To make matters worse, Kazimierz immediately bowed to his parents' wishes and ended the engagement. Somehow Marie swallowed her pride and remained with the Zorawskis. She would not let down her sister Bronya. And while she continued a fitful romance with Kazimierz, it was apparent they would never end up together. As for Kazimierz, he went on to a career as one of Poland's most celebrated mathematicians.

Eyes Toward Paris

After her failed romance, Marie felt isolated and depressed. Relations with the family were civil, but she could not forget their rejection. She wrote despairing letters to her brother, Joseph, expressing her fears that she would never rise above her job as a governess. In the spring of 1889 she finally left the Zorawskis and returned to Warsaw. She took another governess job and struggled to keep up with her studies. Then hopeful signs began to emerge. Her father's new job as director of a reform school allowed him to take over the monthly payments to Bronya in Paris. He also began to pay Marie back for the money she had sent her sister. In 1890 Marie received a life-changing letter from Paris. Bronya, who had recently married, wrote, "And now you, my little Manya. If you can get together a few hundred rubles this year you can come to Paris next year and live with us. . . . You must take this decision, you have been waiting too long."[8] At first Marie was overwhelmed at the prospect of moving to Paris. She replied to her sister with a letter full of doubts. But soon she came to grips with this remarkable opportunity. Her dream of attending university in Paris, which had seemed to fade so badly, was about to come true.

Chapter Two

An Education in Paris

In November 1891 Marie traveled by train to Paris. The forty-hour journey in a noisy, jerking, fourth-class car covered 1,000 miles (1,609 km). She arrived at the glass-roofed station of the Gare du Nord on a chilly morning. Her new home was a city that dated back centuries yet also played host to the latest ideas in art, literature, and science. Wonders confronted her at every turn, from the recently completed Eiffel Tower to the stately spires of the Notre Dame Cathedral. It was a pleasure to simply stroll down the boulevards, with their fancy carriages, fashionable shops, and bustling crowds. Above all, Marie felt a sense of freedom she had never known. She could wander wherever she wished without fear of some Russian official spying on her. She could express herself in Polish or read Polish books if she chose. Paris afforded her the opportunity to truly be herself. "All that I saw and learned that was new delighted me," she wrote later. "It was like a new world opened to me, the world of science, which I was at last permitted to know in all liberty."[9]

Studies at the Sorbonne

At first Marie moved in with her sister Bronya and her sister's new husband, Kazimierz Dluski. Their second-floor apartment on the outskirts of Paris was filled with activity at all hours. Both Bronya and Kazimierz were doctors—Bronya having graduated as one of only three women in a medical school of more than two hundred—and they both saw patients at home in the daytime. At night their home served as a meeting place for a number of lively friends, many of them expatriate Poles. Kazimierz loved to entertain his guests with jokes and stories. Marie felt genuine affection for her brother-in-law and appreciated his hospitality. She particularly liked the warm atmosphere of the apartment, its comfortable secondhand furnishings, and the bookshelves filled with Polish classics. But Kazimierz's constant teasing and banter made it impossible to study. In March 1892 she rented a small place in the Latin Quarter section of Paris. The room lacked electric light and, with only a tiny coal stove, got so cold in the winter that water in a basin froze overnight. Marie would pile all her clothes atop the bedcovers for warmth. However, the room was also cheap and had the additional advantage of being close to the Sorbonne. It was the first of several modest rooms she would rent in the next few years.

In Paris she abandoned the Polish forms of her name: Maria and Manya. She enrolled to study physics and chemistry at the Sorbonne under the name Marie Sklodowska. (Polish surnames for women feature the feminine ending -a.) The Sorbonne was renowned as Europe's most progressive university. It was one of the few schools that accepted females, and its students were given great latitude in their studies. Aside from small fees for introductory tests and diplomas, at-

This depiction of a Paris street scene in the late 19th century captures the city's vibrancy. Moving to Paris in 1891, Marie was delighted with the opportunities her new surroundings afforded her.

tendance at the Sorbonne cost nothing. Marie loved the freedom she enjoyed as a student. Once she had established her qualifications—showing she had graduated from secondary school—she was free to pursue her studies at her own pace. Like the other students, Marie could choose when to attend classes and when to take exams. "The student who comes to France," she noted, "should not expect to find direction towards a utilitarian goal right at the start. The French system consists essentially of awakening the student's confidence in his own abilities and fostering the habit of using them."[10] Marie, with her strong habits of independence, expected to thrive in such a system.

Early Struggles

Once set up in her new quarters, she threw herself into her studies. At first she struggled to understand the lectures at the university. She discovered that her education in Poland had not prepared her as thoroughly as most of the other students in her classes. Her French needed work, particularly with technical terms, and the professors spoke very rapidly. Also, her background in mathematics proved to be somewhat inadequate. Nevertheless, she refused to lose faith. She arrived early for lectures so she could get a seat up front, which helped her hear the professor and see his chalkboard notes more easily. After attending lectures and working in the chemistry laboratory during the day, she would read in the school library each night until closing time at ten o'clock. Then she would return to her room for more study. She kept meals to a minimum to save time and money and relied mainly on bread, fruit, radishes, and eggs. Often she slept no more than four hours a night.

In time her strict regimen began to affect her health. One day a friend saw her collapse on the sidewalk outside her apartment and reported the incident to Bronya and Kazimierz. They hurried over to find Marie reading as usual, with only a few scraps of food in her room.

> *"The student who comes to France should not expect to find direction towards a utilitarian goal right at the start. The French system consists essentially of awakening the student's confidence in his own abilities and fostering the habit of using them."[10]*
>
> —Marie Curie.

Bronya and her husband insisted that Marie accompany them back to their apartment for some home-cooked meals and relaxation. She was grateful for their concern, but as she regained her strength she happily went back to her strenuous routine. In her autobiography, she described her student years:

> This life, painful from certain points of view, had, for all that, a real charm for me. It gave me a very precious sense of liberty and independence. Unknown in Paris, I was lost in the great city, but the feeling of living there alone, taking care of myself without any aid, did not at all depress me. If sometimes I felt lonesome, my usual state of mind was one of calm and great moral satisfaction.[11]

Success and a New Opportunity

With diligent work, Marie managed to overcome her weak points. Her French improved, and she began to grasp the mathematical intricacies necessary for her courses. Nevertheless, most of her professors and fellow students, although polite and helpful, remained skeptical about her prospects. Surely no female could keep up with courses that challenged the best male students. In the summer of 1893, after two years filled with anxiety and effort, Marie finally faced her examinations in physics. After the tests she had to wait several nerve-wracking days for the results. She need not have worried. Not only did she earn her degree in physics—becoming the first woman to accomplish this at the Sorbonne—she finished first in her class. It was a remarkable performance that justified her long hours of study. Her success also proved that being female was no drawback for a dedicated and talented student.

After the physics exams, Marie traveled back to Warsaw to visit her family. Her father hugged her with pride, delighted at her success in his own chosen field. Her brother, Joseph, also offered congratulations. Young women Marie had known in the Floating University praised her for her degree and for the shining example she had set for women's education in general. One friend with connections in Warsaw, a woman named Jadwiga Dydynska, was so enthused that she arranged for Marie to receive a prestigious scholarship worth more

Poland in Paris

Young artists and intellectuals flocked to Paris in the 1890s, keen to experience the most exciting and sophisticated city in Europe. It was the era of optimism, the Belle Époque (or Beautiful Era), with revolutionary changes afoot in art, science, and culture. Among these young people were many Polish émigrés who, like Marie, sought a life of freedom away from the rigid czarist authorities back home. As much as Marie wanted to embrace Paris and the French language, she appreciated the chance to mingle with her fellow Poles at the home of her sister and brother-in-law. In fact, Kazimierz Dluski, her brother-in-law, was among the most colorful Polish exiles in the city. Besides his wit and intellect, he also owned a reputation for daring radical politics. Reportedly, the French Ministry of Foreign Affairs kept files on Dluski from the czarist police in Warsaw. In fact, Marie's father advised her to move out of her sister's house because of the problems she might incur back home after living in the midst of Polish radicals.

Once Marie was out on her own, she still longed for contact with Poland. At Christmas she would join fellow Polish students for banquets, games, and plays. In one such skit, Marie played Poland Breaking Its Bonds. "The severe little student became an unknown woman that night," writes Marie's daughter Ève. "With her transparent skin, her blonde hair and her resolute face with its Slavic cheekbones, she presented to these exiles the picture of their race."

Ève Curie, *Madame Curie*. New York: Da Capo, 2001, pp. 101–102.

than six hundred rubles. Although she found it difficult to leave her father once more, Marie was excited to return to Paris. The scholarship would pay for fifteen months of study, more than enough time for earning her degree in mathematics.

While attending math courses at the Sorbonne, Marie took advantage of another opportunity. A group of factory owners, called the

Society for the Encouragement of National Industry, hired her to conduct a laboratory study of the magnetic properties of various types of steel. Marie was thrilled to secure a paying job, particularly doing scientific research. However, she needed space for her work. One of her professors offered his laboratory, but it proved inadequate for her needs. Then a Polish physicist with whom she was acquainted suggested a possible solution. A colleague of his was a scientist and teacher at the School of Physics and Chemistry. He might have a suitable workroom for her. Marie promptly set up a meeting with this scientist, whose name was Pierre Curie.

A Momentous Meeting

As it turned out, Marie's physicist friend was mistaken about Pierre Curie's lab facilities at the school. Curie worked in cramped quarters himself. Nevertheless, he took an interest in this bright, charming young woman from Poland. At their first meeting, the two fell into a friendly conversation. Marie asked Pierre his opinion about certain scientific matters concerning magnetism, his field of expertise. Soon they moved on to social and humanitarian topics that interested them both. They quickly discovered that, despite their different backgrounds, they shared many of the same ideas. Marie attributed this to the similar moral atmosphere of their childhood homes. In her autobiography, she remembered her first impression of Pierre: "He seemed to me very young, though he was at that time thirty-five years old. I was struck by the open expression of his face and by the slight suggestion of detachment in his whole attitude. His speech, rather slow and deliberate, his simplicity, and his smile, at once grave and youthful, inspired confidence."[12]

> "He seemed to me very young, though he was at that time thirty-five years old. . . . His speech, rather slow and deliberate, his simplicity, and his smile, at once grave and youthful, inspired confidence."[12]
>
> —Marie Curie.

Pierre's confidence owed something to the fact that he was already established as an expert on magnetism. He had been born in Paris and raised in a household devoted to liberal—even radical—political ideas.

Marie met her future husband, physicist Pierre Curie, when he provided her with work space in his lab. The two quickly discovered they had many similar ideas and interests despite their different backgrounds.

His father, Eugène, was a physician who had treated the wounds of street fighters in the revolutions of 1848 and 1871. Dr. Curie threw his support behind republicans who sought a more democratic approach to government. Pierre and his older brother, Jacques, were educated by their parents at home, where lessons could be less regimented and the boys could take advantage of their father's large library. Dr. Curie also took his sons on long outings in the country, where he would point out details of the natural world and encourage the boys to be

Pierre Curie and Piezoelectricity

Pierre Curie's research with his wife, Marie, on radioactivity would help bring about the atomic age. However, his work on piezoelectricity, a subtler and less-known phenomenon, has also had an impact on modern technology. Pierre and his brother, Jacques, used their study of the piezoelectric effect to create a quartz electrometer, an extremely sensitive device for detecting electric currents in the air. For years this was the only practical outcome of the brothers' research, partly because the math related to it was so complex.

It was left to other scientists to find new uses for the piezoelectric effect. In 1910 Woldemar Voigt published a detailed analysis of the subject, describing twenty types of natural crystal with piezoelectric potential. Voigt's work led to many inventions. In 1917 Paul Langevin, Pierre's student, employed thin quartz crystals to create an ultrasonic transducer, or sonar device, for submarines. It emitted a high-frequency pulse underwater and measured depth by timing the returning echo. Certain automobiles today have similar devices to detect the distance from the rear bumper to any obstacles. Research during World War II revealed ways to greatly increase the piezoelectric effect. This resulted in a flood of new applications. "If you've got a quartz watch, piezoelectricity is what helps it keep regular time," explains technology expert Chris Woodford. "If you're a bit of an audiophile and like listening to music on vinyl, your gramophone would have been using piezoelectricity to 'read' the sounds from your LP records."

Chris Woodford, "Piezoelectricity," Explain That Stuff!, July 14, 2014. www.explainthatstuff.com.

perceptive about their surroundings. This eccentric education proved effective. At sixteen, Pierre easily passed the entrance exams at the Sorbonne, and two years later he earned his master's degree in physics. However, financial woes not unlike those that affected Marie's family forced Pierre to forego his plans to get his doctorate. Instead, he settled for a job as a lab instructor. It was in this capacity that he was able to equip Marie with a small working space for her new job. The two of them began to see each other nearly every day.

Pierre Curie's Work on Magnetism

Marie soon learned that Pierre, for all his modesty and indifference to money, was a well-respected scientist. Many of his experiments were carried out with his brother, Jacques, who worked in the Sorbonne mineralogy laboratory. The brothers had spent years studying phenomena connected to the theory of electromagnetism and ways of generating electricity with magnetic force. Their particular interest was called the piezoelectric effect (from the Greek word *piezein*, meaning "to press"). They had begun with experiments on how a change in temperature in various crystals could generate the potential for electricity. They found that by subjecting crystals such as quartz, topaz, and cane sugar to mechanical stress, or squeezing, the result was indeed an electric potential. To measure the amount of this potential, they invented a sensitive device called the piezoelectric quartz electrometer.

Shortly after the Curie brothers' discovery, their mentor, the mathematician Gabriel Lippmann, theorized that the converse of the piezoelectric effect should also be true. Applying an electric field to a crystal should cause the crystalline material to change shape, as if it were being compressed. The Curie brothers were able to confirm Lippmann's theory. Pierre described their work in scientific journals that were read by scientists the world over. He and his brother initiated research that led to many breakthroughs in related areas, including the invention of sonar for tracking the movements of submarines. Decades later, consumer items from inkjet printers to quartz watches would operate according to the piezoelectric effect discovered by the Curie brothers. Pierre's expertise on crystals and electricity would also prove beneficial to his and Marie's later experiments. He always touted the incremental nature of scientific research. As he observed in an 1894 letter to Marie, "[In science] we can aspire to accomplish something. . . . Every discovery, however small, is a permanent gain."[13]

From Colleagues to Spouses

Along with her commissioned work, Marie continued her studies in mathematics. In 1894 she obtained her degree, this time finishing second overall in her class. That summer she again returned to Warsaw for vacation and traveled to Switzerland with her family. She enjoyed the time spent with her father and siblings, but she could not hide her confused feelings. For the second time in her life, Marie was in love.

Seeing Pierre so frequently, Marie had overcome her reluctance to be romantically involved again. Despite the difference in their ages—Pierre was almost ten years older—she began to develop strong feelings for this brilliant, cultured Frenchman. It was such a pleasure being with someone devoted to science and research, someone who shared her passion for the life of the mind. They were also linked in

Newlyweds Pierre and Marie Curie pose for a photograph. Their honeymoon was spent bicycling through the Brittany region of France.

another way. Like Marie, Pierre had suffered heartache and all but given up on romance. Fifteen years before, a female companion of his had died. Since then the women he met had invariably disappointed him, lacking any interest in science. Then Marie had appeared, lively and attractive and equally drawn to the work that he loved. Marie expressed it best when she wrote, "Our work drew us closer and closer until we were both convinced that neither of us could find a better life companion."[14] Before she left for Warsaw, Pierre had surprised her by proposing marriage. Now, as she accompanied her family to Switzerland, his love letters followed her. He wrote: "It would be a fine thing, in which I hardly dare believe, to pass our lives near each other, hypnotized by our dreams; your patriotic dream, our humanitarian dream and our scientific dream."[15] He urged Marie to pursue her doctorate in Paris. Her plans of remaining in Warsaw to teach and care for her father began to give way.

> *"It would be a fine thing, in which I hardly dare believe, to pass our lives near each other, hypnotized by our dreams; your patriotic dream, our humanitarian dream and our scientific dream."*[15]
>
> —Pierre Curie, in a letter to Marie.

When Marie decided to return to Paris in the fall, Pierre was ecstatic. Nonetheless, she wavered about the future, hesitant to abandon her father, her family and friends, and Poland. She had always intended to marry a Polish patriot like herself. Her brother, Joseph, offered his support, assuring her that following her dreams and marrying a Frenchman who loved her was certainly no betrayal. A few months later she wrote her family to announce her coming marriage to Pierre Curie. The modest ceremony took place in July 1895, in the Paris suburb where Pierre's parents lived. Afterward, the couple took a train to the coast of Brittany in northwest France. Their honeymoon consisted of a leisurely tour of the fields and rocky headlands atop their wedding presents: two new bicycles.

Chapter Three

Discovering Radium

After their honeymoon, Marie and Pierre Curie moved into a small apartment in Paris. The couple immediately settled into a demanding routine. Three months before their wedding, Pierre had received his doctoral degree in physics, which also brought a promotion to a full professorship at the university and a higher salary. Now, in addition to teaching, he was giving lectures on magnetism and crystals and continuing his research in this area. Marie returned to her commission work on steel while also studying for exams to become a teacher. What little time she had left each month was devoted to housework and balancing the accounts. On September 12, 1897, Marie gave birth to their first child, Irène—attended by her physician father-in-law, Eugène. When Eugène's wife died soon thereafter, Marie, Pierre, and the baby moved into a new house with Eugène. Pierre's father insisted on caring for Irène while her parents went to work. This freed the busy couple to consider another exciting possibility. Marie could pursue her own doctorate in physics.

A Subject for Research

To obtain this most prestigious of degrees, Marie had to choose a topic for her dissertation. With her inquisitive mind, she spent hours poring over the pages of scientific journals. Finally, she settled on a subject related to two recent discoveries in physics. In December 1895 the German physicist Wilhelm Roentgen had passed electrical current from an induction coil through a glass vacuum tube. When he covered the tube in black paper and turned out the lights, the rays passed through the paper to illuminate a screen smeared with fluorescent material. Roentgen found that the rays from the vacuum tube could penetrate certain materials but not others. For example, the rays projected an image on a photographic plate of his wife's hand, penetrating the translucent flesh to show the opaque bones beneath and the ring on her finger. Roentgen called these mysterious rays X-rays, for the unknown variable X in math equations. Science historian Hannah Waters says Roentgen's discovery had an immediate impact on everyday life:

> His discovery transformed medicine almost overnight. Within a year, the first radiology department opened in a Glasgow hospital, and the department head produced the first pictures

The work of German physicist Wilhelm Roentgen, including an X-ray photograph he made of his wife's hand similar to this one, inspired Marie Curie to research radiation. She was also influenced in this pursuit by the work of French physicist Antoine-Henri Becquerel, which led her to focus her studies around the element uranium.

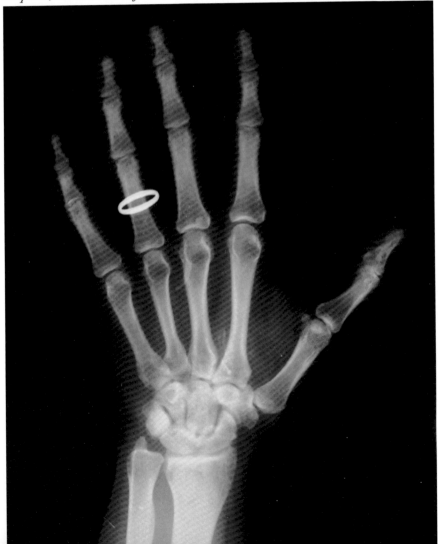

of a kidney stone and a penny lodged in a child's throat. Shortly after, an American physiologist used X-rays to trace food making its way through the digestive system. The public also embraced the new technology—even carnival barkers touted the wondrous rays that allowed viewing of one's own skeleton.[16]

Although scientists were as fascinated by X-rays as the public, they also were puzzled. The discovery raised many questions. For example, if atoms were solid units, how was this new radiation able to penetrate them?

Early in 1896 the French physicist Antoine-Henri Becquerel made another discovery having to do with radiation. Fascinated by X-rays, Becquerel was conducting his own experiments with fluorescence. He intended to expose a compound of uranium crystals to sunlight and then place it on photographic plates, expecting the sun's energy to cause the compound to fluoresce and expose the plates. Since the day was cloudy, Becquerel stored the uranium compound with the plates for later use. However, when he went back to retrieve the photographic plates, he found that they had been exposed anyway, bearing the clear silhouettes of some objects, including a Maltese cross, stored with the uranium samples. As science writer Carolyn Gramling observes, "Stimulation of the crystals by sunlight before or during the experiment, it seemed, was not necessary to produce the images—suggesting that the crystals themselves were emitting radiation, without external stimulation."[17] On March 1, 1896, Becquerel presented his discovery to the Académie des sciences (French Academy of Sciences) in Paris. He went on to show that the rays he had found—which became known as Becquerel rays—could penetrate materials just as X-rays did. Unlike X-rays, however, they could be deflected by a magnetic field, indicating they contained electrically charged particles. This radiation was something entirely new.

> "The public also embraced the new technology [of X-rays]— even carnival barkers touted the wondrous rays that allowed viewing of one's own skeleton."[16]
>
> —Science historian Hannah Waters.

Becquerel and the Curies

The respected French physicist Antoine-Henri Becquerel played a major role in Marie Curie's career as a scientist. His discovery of uranium rays inspired Marie to pursue research on radioactivity. And through the years, Becquerel's work and that of Marie and Pierre Curie became linked, not only among scientists, but in the news media. This association culminated in the 1903 Nobel Prize in Physics, which was shared, unequally, among the three scientists—Becquerel received half the prize himself. Behind the scenes the relationship between Becquerel and the Curies was anything but smooth.

Becquerel came from a family of scientists. He drew his interest in fluorescence and phosphorescence from his father, who had studied these phenomena at length and left Antoine-Henri the minerals and compounds from his work. Antoine-Henri's breakthrough with uranium rays cemented his reputation as a scientist. Yet it was Becquerel's former student, Marie, who perceived the significance of uranium rays, or radioactivity. At first Becquerel was generous with the Curies, helping them organize their finances and offering his recommendations for jobs. Later, as the Curies gained fame, the older scientist adopted a condescending attitude toward them. In 1911, when an international board established units of measurement for radioactivity, Marie got some revenge. "One curie equals 37 billion becquerels," notes science writer Wayne Biddle. "Perhaps this would please Madame Curie, who never much liked the imperious Professor Henri Becquerel."

Wayne Biddle, *A Field Guide to Radiation*. New York: Penguin, 2012, pp. 74–75.

When Marie read about Becquerel's experiments with uranium, she knew she had found the perfect subject for her doctoral research. It was a chance to enter a field not already overrun by other scientists, a chance to make a name for herself. Pierre agreed that she should begin her study of uranium rays at once.

The Path to Discovery

For her PhD work, Marie needed a new laboratory. The best she and Pierre could do was a small, damp storeroom at the School of Physics and Chemistry where he taught. She emptied the cramped space of clutter and set up her equipment as best she could on the rickety tables. One special instrument gave her an advantage over Becquerel's approach. Instead of using photographic plates to register the presence of radiation in a rough way, she employed the electrometer invented by Pierre and his brother. The device enabled her to measure the electrical effect of uranium rays with great precision. This was important because Becquerel had suggested that uranium creates a small electrical current, a theory confirmed by a Scottish scientist, Lord Kelvin. Marie writes in her account of the study:

> *"In order to go beyond the results reached by Becquerel, it was necessary to employ a precise quantitative method. The phenomenon that best lent itself to measurement was the conductibility produced in the air by uranium rays."*[18]
>
> —Marie Curie.

In order to go beyond the results reached by Becquerel, it was necessary to employ a precise quantitative method. The phenomenon that best lent itself to measurement was the conductibility produced in the air by uranium rays. This phenomenon, which is called ionization, is produced also by X-rays and investigation of it in connection with them had made known its principal characteristics.[18]

Marie spent several days learning to use the sensitive electrometer until its operation became second nature to her.

Satisfied with her modest laboratory, Marie got to work. Her first enquiries concerned whether uranium produced stronger rays in certain physical or chemical states than others. She pulverized uranium into dust, mixed it with other elements, exposed it to sunlight, and tested it wet and dry. Although the damp air in the storeroom tended to weaken the electric charge, the electrometer consistently showed that the same amount of uranium, in whatever state or mixture, produced the same amount of current. This confirmed Becquerel's idea that greater portions of uranium produced more intense rays. However, Marie next used her talent for analysis to leap beyond Becquerel at one stroke. Her insight would prove crucial to the study of atomic structure.

Investigating Radioactivity

Marie's hypothesis was that the radiation emitted by uranium resulted from some inherent property of its atoms, not from their arrangement. The recent discovery of the electron by British physicist Joseph John Thomson in 1897 had indicated that atoms were not indivisible units as previously thought. Marie's insight into the nature of uranium rays brought forth many new questions about the makeup of atoms. Perhaps

Curie used these instruments in her research; at far right is the electrometer that Pierre invented with his brother, Jacques. This device enabled Marie to precisely measure the electrical effects of uranium rays.

The Radium Fad

"It was a pity that radium did not seem to have any practical uses," Marie Curie's father wrote to her in 1902. The properties of radium, an element isolated from pitchblende ore by Marie and Pierre in 1898, had yet to be thoroughly investigated. The Curies themselves handled tubes of radium salts every day, and the dangerous radiation left them with burns on their fingers and a persistent aching fatigue. But the element, with its eerie bluish glow, captured the public's imagination much as the discovery of X-rays had a few years before. Companies began to add radium to their products to be fashionable. Hair dyes with radium promised to return graying hair to its original color. Radium-laced face creams claimed to produce glowingly healthy skin, and radium hair lotions touted long-lasting curls. Even toothpastes and shampoos advertised the benefits of radium. The element was promoted as a miracle cure for all sorts of conditions, from arthritis to mental illness.

Radium was also used to create glow-in-the-dark clock dials. Young women at the United States Radium factory in Orange, New Jersey, would paint the dials, forming their brush tips into fine points with their lips before dipping the brushes into the radium paint. Months later several of the women began to develop serious symptoms, including large tumors on their jaws. It is not known how many of the women died from their exposure. News stories about their condition helped raise awareness about the actual dangers of radium.

Quoted in Philip Steele, *Marie Curie: The Woman Who Changed the Course of Science.* Washington, DC: National Geographic Society, 2006.

there were other particles like electrons that caused radiation. The Curies wavered over whether the rays originated in uranium atoms or were the result of cosmic radiation from space that somehow became trapped in uranium atoms and radiated from them. At any rate, Marie did not let herself get bogged down in speculation, focusing instead on obtaining proof for her hypothesis. She decided to study other metals and minerals to see if they too emitted rays that created electrical current in the air—a phenomenon she dubbed *radioactivity* for its apparent similarity to radio waves. Pierre, intrigued by his wife's findings, joined her in this research.

Over several weeks they tested many different elements. Marie obtained ores from geological museums, and certain chemists, learning of the Curies' work, donated extremely rare samples. One element, thorium, produced rays much like uranium. Then Marie began to focus on uranium ores. She was startled to discover that two of these, pitchblende and chalcolite, produced much higher readings of radioactivity *after* the uranium had been extracted. At first Marie assumed that the electrometer was faulty, but repeated tests confirmed the readings. The Curies pondered the meaning of Marie's discovery. Pitchblende, an ore mined in the border region of Germany and Austria, was thought to be a negligible by-product of uranium mining, worthless once the uranium was removed. It consisted of some thirty chemical elements and compounds. Marie knew there had to be something hidden within the ore that was strongly radioactive. She suspected that the rays were produced by a previously unknown element, the discovery of which would certainly be a tremendous achievement. And it would be all the more remarkable proceeding not from an expensively equipped Parisian laboratory but from a cramped, converted storeroom with a leaky ceiling. Nevertheless, despite the exciting prospects, Marie kept her composure. She knew that any potential breakthrough would require long hours of patient work.

Identifying a New Element

The task of extracting each separate element for testing proved to be a challenge. Since neither Marie nor Pierre was a chemist, they sought the advice of Gustave Bémont, a chemistry instructor at a municipal school. The work was difficult, and the Curies also had to deal with inadequate facilities and lack of money and personnel. Marie and Pierre were searching for an element whose chemical properties were unknown. Its presence could be traced only by its radioactivity. It was like seeking a hidden coin in a large auditorium while blindfolded.

To isolate sources of radioactivity, the Curies devised an ingenious new method of chemical analysis. They separated out from the pitchblende each of its known elements and then measured the radioactivity of each element with the electrometer. The separation process included heating, treatment with strong acids, sifting, and other forms of extraction. After each separation, Marie performed a novel step of her own. "Marie devised an elegant chemical procedure known as fractional crystallization," explains Curie's biographer Denise Ham, who compares the procedure to making rock candy. "Fractional crystallization is more difficult than making candy, because the chemist must know everything about the elements he is dealing with, the crystals that will form, at what temperature that formation will take place, the atomic weights of the elements that are being boiled, which elements will crystallize first, and so on."[19] Marie's efforts inside her makeshift shed were also a crash course in advanced chemical analysis.

Each separate product was carefully tested for radioactivity. As elements were eliminated one by one, the remaining substance showed increasing levels of radioactivity. Yet the radioactivity was apparently produced by trace elements in tiny amounts. "Since the composition of [pitchblende] was known through very careful chemical analysis," Marie later explained, "we could expect to find, at a maximum, 1 per cent of new substance. The result of our experiment proved that there were in reality new radioactive elements in pitchblende, but that their proportion did not reach even a millionth per cent!"[20]

Eventually, the Curies isolated a sample that contained mostly bismuth, a brittle, white, crystalline metal. The sample produced levels of radioactivity three hundred to four hundred times greater than pure uranium. The Curies could not find a procedure to separate the sample's active substance from the bismuth. Marie realized that the unknown element they were seeking was tightly fused to the bismuth and therefore had to be chemically very similar.

At this point, Marie enlisted the help of Eugène Demarçay, a Parisian friend and expert in the field of spectroscopy. The spectroscope, invented in 1814, is a prism-based instrument that separates light into its different wavelengths. It can reveal the characteristic wavelengths of light for each element by projecting them as a pattern of lines. Demarçay used his spectroscope to produce faint spectral lines from the bismuth residue. Demarçay who could recognize the spectroscope pattern for every known element, was astonished. The chemical fingerprint for the Curies' sample was different from that of every element previously known. Marie and Pierre had indeed found a new element. Marie decided to call it polonium, in honor of her native Poland. In July 1898 the Curies published a paper on their discovery, titled "On a New Radioactive Substance Contained in Pitchblende." The article introduced the scientific world to a new element and a new word, *radioactive*. Only five months had elapsed since Marie first detected radioactivity in pitchblende.

Another Major Discovery

Inspired by their breakthrough, Marie and Pierre continued their analysis of pitchblende. Their work convinced them that there were actually two strongly radioactive elements in the ore. The second was fused with barium in the same way that polonium was bound up with bismuth. It was also significantly more radioactive than polonium. In December 1898 the Curies' notified the French Academy of Sciences about their discovery of this second element. They named it radium, based on the Latin word for *ray*.

The yellow lines of this magnified image show the tracks of particles emitted by a single speck of radium. A million times more radioactive than uranium, radium was discovered by Marie and Pierre Curie in 1898.

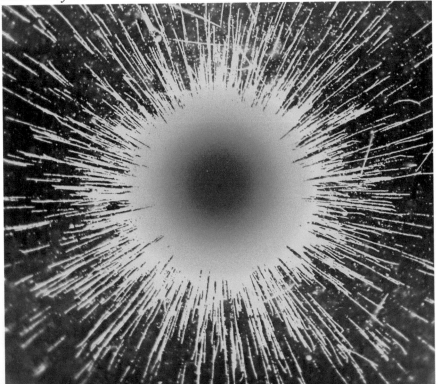

The scientific world regarded the Curies' discovery with great interest but also with a certain amount of skepticism. Some questioned Marie's contribution simply because she was a woman. Pierre's aloofness from the science community also worked against them. Marie saw that further work would be needed to convince the skeptics. "In our opinion, there could be no doubt of the existence of these new elements," she wrote, "but to make chemists admit their existence, it was necessary to isolate them."[21] The problem was that polonium and radium occur only as traces in pitchblende. To produce larger quantities suitable for testing and weighing would require a huge amount of ore. For their research, the Curies succeeded in obtaining, for a reasonable price, several tons of pitchblende slag from the Austrian government. The supposedly worthless residue, stripped of its uranium and still mixed with pine needles from the forest dumping ground, would prove to be a boon to science. Marie and Pierre set about isolating the new elements by chemical means.

Labor-Intensive Years

This phase of the Curies' work was akin to an industrial-scale project. To perform their chemical separations on tons of ore, they moved into an abandoned shed across a courtyard from Marie's original workroom. This wooden shed with its leaky glass roof was stifling in summer and bone chilling in winter. It contained a few worn tables of pine and a balky cast-iron stove, but no hoods or fans to carry off poisonous fumes from the chemical treatments. An open window provided the only ventilation. Wilhelm Ostwald, a visiting German chemist, was astonished to see the state of the Curies' laboratory: "It was a cross between a stable and a potato-cellar, and, if I had not seen the worktable with the chemical apparatus, I would have thought it a practical joke."[22]

Marie and Pierre carried out their arduous labor with little thought for their surroundings or health. Marie would perform the chemical separations while Pierre took careful measurements after each step. For months she boiled pitchblende with various chemicals in a massive cauldron, stirring the sludge with a heavy iron rod. When the mixture was ready, she would carry it out to the courtyard and perform the final steps in the open air. Neither rain nor snow slowed the process. At day's end she was woozy with fatigue. Conditions inside the shed were much worse than the Curies suspected. Radium residues lay openly in flasks or bottles on the tables and shelves. Marie attested to the joy she and Pierre felt at seeing the bluish glow of these faintly luminous substances when returning to the dark shed. Both Curies suffered burns from constantly handling radioactive material. In addition, the shed doubtless contained dangerous levels of radon, a radioactive gas. Marie's makeshift laboratory, soon to become iconic in scientific lore, was also a contaminated death trap.

Each batch of ore yielded only a tiny fraction of radium salts. It took three years of intensive work to produce 0.0035 ounces of pure radium chloride—one-tenth of a gram. The Curies failed to extract even that amount of polonium due to the element's rapid decay, a characteristic that scientists would discover only later. Yet Marie and Pierre had affirmed the existence of the new elements and established themselves as experts on radioactive materials. News stories fed public interest in radium as a possible source of illumination and energy. The tabloids focused on the Curies' remarkable partnership and their humble workplace. Marie would always remember the "miserable old shed" and the satisfactions of working there with her husband. "I shall never be able to express the joy of the untroubled quietness of this atmosphere of research," she wrote later, "and the excitement of actual progress with the confident hope of still better results. The feeling of discouragement that sometimes came after some unsuccessful toil did not last long and gave way to renewed activity. We had happy moments devoted to a quiet discussion of our work, walking around our shed."[23] These were the happiest years of her life.

> "[The Curies' laboratory] was a cross between a stable and a potato-cellar, and, if I had not seen the worktable with the chemical apparatus, I would have thought it a practical joke."[22]
>
> —German chemist Wilhelm Ostwald.

Chapter Four

A Tragic Death

By 1903 Marie and Pierre had secured a place for themselves in the history of science. Scientists around the world had read of their work and regarded their achievement with great respect. Only in France had the reaction been muted. In 1898, when the Sorbonne had held an election for a prestigious post, one for which Pierre's scientific work seemed an ideal qualification, the professors had expressed their dislike of him by voting him down. Perhaps the professors interpreted Pierre's quiet manner and stubborn independence as arrogance. Regardless, despite his growing reputation, Pierre made barely enough to support the family. In 1900 Marie had taken an extra job teaching physics at a leading college for women in order to bring in more money. Two years later Pierre was again rejected when he applied to become a member of the French Academy of Sciences. This disappointment, along with the death of Marie's father in May 1902, dampened some of the Curies' excitement about their radium research. Later that year, however, when the University of Geneva in Switzerland offered Pierre an advanced position and better salary, the French establishment finally roused itself to reward the increasingly famous Curies. The Sorbonne, pressed into action by the great mathematician Henri Poincaré, offered Pierre its chair in physics, a move that helped ease some of his and Marie's money concerns.

The First Female Doctorate

With the Curies' financial situation improved, Marie focused on the next large step in her academic career. On June 25, 1903, she defended her doctoral thesis on radioactivity before a panel of professors at the Sorbonne. She was the first woman ever to undergo such an examination. The panel consisted of distinguished scientists. Of its three members, two would go on to win a Nobel Prize for science, including

Gabriel Lippmann, a physicist and Marie's former teacher. Marie answered each question about her paper thoroughly and with impressive poise. At times she resorted to writing and drawing on a blackboard to explain a difficult point. The professors' verdict was unanimous: Marie was now a doctor of physics. Lippmann spoke for the committee when he observed that Marie's findings represented the most outstanding contribution to science ever made in a doctoral thesis.

That evening Paul Langevin, a research colleague, arranged a celebratory dinner in Marie's honor. Among the guests was the British physicist Ernest Rutherford, who was visiting Paris and wanted to meet Marie and her husband. In 1899 Rutherford had made his own breakthrough in the study of radioactivity, discovering alpha and beta rays in uranium radiation. The next year he had suggested that radioactive decay is actually the process of one element changing into another. The Curies had offered assistance by sending him highly radioactive materials for his work. Upon finally meeting Marie, the gregarious Rutherford found this slight, intense Polish woman to be friendly but reserved. He had dropped by the municipal school before arriving for dinner, and he teased her about the simple shed where she carried out

British physicist Ernest Rutherford studied radioactivity at the same time as the Curies. Working independently from each other, he and the couple made similar discoveries.

her research. "You know," he said, "it must be dreadful not to have a laboratory to play around in."[24] After dinner Rutherford accompanied the party into the garden, where Pierre had prepared a surprise. Biographer Nanny Fröman describes the scene:

> When they had all sat down, [Pierre] drew from his waistcoat pocket a little tube, partly coated with zinc sulfide, which contained a quantity of radium salt in solution. Suddenly the tube became luminous, lighting up the darkness, and the group stared at the display in wonder, quietly and solemnly. But in the light from the tube, Rutherford saw that Pierre's fingers were scarred and inflamed and that he was finding it hard to hold the tube.[25]

Rutherford noticed the same kinds of cracks and burn scars on Marie's fingers. It was evidence of the toll the couple's research was taking on their health. Yet Rutherford, like the Curies, failed to perceive—or simply ignored—the true hazards of working with radioactive samples. He would go on to make several groundbreaking discoveries related to atomic structure and particle physics. Over the years Ernest Rutherford and Marie Curie enjoyed a cordial relationship of mutual respect.

A Remarkable Nobel Prize

The Curies were anxious to resume their own research on radium and its effects. The summer months had been difficult. In August 1903 Marie suffered a miscarriage. Pierre experienced terrible pain from sores caused by contact with radium, sometimes lying awake all night. Yet by December he had settled into his teaching duties at the Sorbonne, and Marie had obtained a position there as head of research. One day news arrived that the Curies, along with their colleague Antoine-Henri Becquerel, had been awarded the Nobel Prize in Physics. The Nobel Prize was the legacy of Alfred Nobel, a Swedish chemist who had invented dynamite and set up the prize committee to honor advances in science and medicine. The awards had begun only in 1901, but the committee was known to evaluate candidates with great care, and the Nobel Prize already had earned a high reputation.

Nonetheless, the Curies' prize was not without controversy. The French Academy of Sciences had originally nominated only Pierre and Becquerel for the award, assuming, with the chauvinism of the time, that Marie's contribution to the work on radioactivity must have been negligible. Months earlier the Swedish mathematician Magnus Gösta Mittag-Leffler, a supporter of women in science, had written to Pierre about the situation. Pierre made his viewpoint clear in his reply: "If it is true that one is seriously thinking about me [for the Nobel Prize], I very much wish to be considered together with Madame Curie with respect to our research on radioactive bodies."[26] Ultimately, the Nobel committee included Marie among the recipients, making her the first woman to be awarded the prize. The Curies' story drew plenty of attention from the world press, which previously had shown little interest in the Nobel committee's science awards. Reporters turned out reams of copy on Madame Curie, the brilliant woman physicist.

At the suggestion of chemists on the nominating board, no mention was made of the Curies' discovery of polonium and radium. The citation focused on their work with Becquerel rays. This paved the way for the Curies someday to win a separate prize in chemistry. However, cynics whispered that the real reason for this omission was the doubtful existence of these new elements. It was more evidence of Marie and Pierre's uphill battle against some of science's entrenched authorities.

The Curies welcomed their half of the prize money attached to the award. It helped pay for the research on pitchblende and enabled them to hire a lab assistant. Nonetheless, all the publicity and interviews quickly became a burden to the quiet couple. The Nobel presentation had to be postponed due to Marie's pregnancy and general weakness—the latter, experienced also by Pierre, probably the result of radiation poisoning. On December 6, 1904, Marie had a second

> *"When they had all sat down, [Pierre] drew from his waistcoat pocket a little tube . . . which contained a quantity of radium salt in solution. . . . In the light from the tube, Rutherford saw that Pierre's fingers were scarred and inflamed and that he was finding it hard to hold the tube."[25]*
>
> —Biographer Nanny Fröman.

47

daughter, Ève Denise Curie. Six months later the Curies journeyed to Sweden to accept the Nobel Prize. The glittering ceremony seemed distant from their homely shed in more than just miles.

Commercial Prospects for Radium

The breakthrough discoveries made in the Curies' shed were already attracting commercial interest. Radium, the substance that glowed and produced its own heat energy, seemed to have exciting possibilities, despite the difficulty involved in extracting it. It might lead to a new source of energy or a novel form of illumination. Pierre's experiments had suggested radium could damage living cells—although he was slow to acknowledge its effects on his own tissues. Reading about his work, physicians soon recognized radium's potential as a tool to fight cancer. Marie and Pierre also saw that radium could be misused. "One may imagine," Pierre had announced in his speech to the Royal Swedish Academy of Sciences in Stockholm, "that in criminal hands radium might become very dangerous, and here we may ask ourselves if humanity has anything to gain by learning the secrets of nature." But then he added, "I am among those who think, with Nobel, that humanity will obtain more good than evil from the new discoveries."[27] The Curies' ambivalence foreshadowed concerns about atomic energy that would emerge in later decades.

> *"I am among those who think, with Nobel, that humanity will obtain more good than evil from the new discoveries."*[27]
>
> —Pierre Curie.

Marie and Pierre did not object to expanding the production of radium. They entered an agreement with the French industrialist Émile Armet de Lisle to produce radium salts in a factory. The deal benefited both parties. Armet de Lisle could count on the Curies' expertise in extracting the element and gained prestige from their Nobel reputation. The Curies acquired a valuable source of radium for their research without the backbreaking labor. Marie Curie would continue to work with Émile Armet de Lisle until his death in 1928. As for the radium industry, it would soon spread to many countries, with several factories built in the United States. Demand at hospitals and clinics alone made the substance a valuable commodity.

Marie Curie poses with her daughters, Ève and Irène, approximately five years after winning the Nobel Prize in 1903. By the time she was awarded the Nobel, Curie was exhibiting telltale signs of radiation poisoning, including fatigue.

One thing the Curies did not insist on was patent rights to their extraction process. They preferred to focus on the study of radium for its scientific value. Had they been otherwise inclined, they might have made millions. (The radium they had already produced was probably worth more than 1 million French francs.) Instead, content with modest salaries, they took a family vacation to the French countryside and then returned to the Sorbonne and the scientific work they both loved.

The Nature of Radiation

At roughly the same time, the Curies and the British physicist Ernest Rutherford made an important discovery about the nature of radiation. The three scientists found that there are actually three types of radiation, and that some are not rays at all but tiny particles. Alpha particles are emitted from an atom's nucleus with high energy, but this energy quickly dissipates. An alpha particle cannot penetrate anything thicker than paper or tinfoil. Beta particles, which are actually electrons with a negative electric charge, can penetrate deeper, damaging tissue and causing cancer. Gamma radiation, which actually consists of rays or electromagnetic waves, can penetrate more deeply than either alpha or beta particles—even through a yard of concrete. Marie's observations about the different types of radiation led to the basic understanding of radioactivity.

Working with chemist Frederick Soddy, Rutherford made another crucial discovery about radiation. As radioactive elements emit radiation in particles or waves, they decay, or lose energy. They actually change into a related element, called an isotope. This disintegration process proceeds from stage to stage at a predictable rate. Every radioactive isotope has its own half-life—the specific period of time in which half the nuclei in the isotope will decay. For example, the element radium has a half-life of sixteen hundred years, which is short enough to produce intense radioactivity. Rutherford's discovery enabled scientists to date ancient rocks and fossils with great precision using mathematical calculations. The technique, called radiocarbon dating, has revealed the age of the earth to be about 4.5 billion years.

A Tragic Accident

In April 1906 Pierre Curie was finally getting back to a regular routine after the uproar related to the Nobel Prize. He and Marie were blissfully happy raising their two daughters. He had finally gained acceptance into the French Academy of Sciences after years of being snubbed. The Sorbonne had provided him the long-promised lab facilities he needed for his work. His tireless support for Marie's scientific achievements, including in his Nobel speech, had helped her earn a solid position as well as the respect of Europe's top scientists. Now he wanted only to be left to the privacy of the laboratory with Marie.

On April 19, after a morning spent in the lab, Pierre made his way to his publisher's office to get the proofs for an article he had written. He raised his umbrella against a heavy rain for the short walk. Arriving to find the doors locked due to a workers' strike, he hurried back across the street, no doubt distracted as usual with thoughts of his work. He did not see the approach of a heavy horse-drawn wagon. The horses reared and he was knocked to the pavement. One wheel rolled over him, crushing his skull. Pierre died instantly.

A crowd gathered as police identified the celebrated scientist from some cards in his pocket. The head of the Sorbonne directed the police to the Curie home, accompanied by Jean Perrin, a physicist and family friend. Instead of Marie, they found Pierre's father, sitting with baby Ève. Told of the accident, the stricken old man immediately blamed it on his son's preoccupation with his research. It was evening before Marie learned the news. Determined to be strong, she composed herself and made the necessary arrangements and notifications. Her only breakdown occurred with the arrival of Pierre's brother and fellow scientist, Jacques, the following day.

Newspapers worldwide carried the story of Pierre Curie's tragic death. Telegrams and letters poured in, and many prominent scientists paid tribute to Pierre. At the funeral on the outskirts of Paris, Marie placed a photograph of herself inside the coffin. In her journal, she described the moment: "I put my head against the coffin and spoke to you. I told you that I loved you and that I had always loved you with all my heart. . . . Something came to me, something like a calm and an intuition that I would yet find the courage to live."[28] She and Pierre had dabbled in spiritualism and séances—oddly perhaps for a couple devoted to science—and she held out hope that her husband's spirit might contact her somehow.

Afterward Jacques told Marie that the French government had proposed a lifetime pension for her and the children. Although she appreciated the offer, Marie rejected it at once. She announced that she was fully capable of supporting herself and her family. Alone with her thoughts, however, she seemed more uncertain. She was thirty-nine years old and felt cast adrift. At one stroke she had lost her husband, lover, friend, confidant, supporter, and invaluable research partner. "Crushed by the blow," she wrote later, "I did not feel able to face the future. I could not forget, however, what my husband used to say, that even deprived of him, I ought to continue my work."[29]

Carrying On Alone

A proposal regarding future scientific work met with more interest from Marie. The dean of the Sorbonne offered her Pierre's position in the physics department (although not his official chair, for which Marie, as a woman, was deemed unsuitable). She hesitated at first, but agreed to take the job. For her first lecture, on November 5, 1906—the first by a female lecturer in the school's history—the hall was filled with reporters, photographers, fellow scientists, and former students. The audience stood and applauded when Marie appeared wearing her usual plain dark dress. Instead of beginning, as was customary, with praise for her predecessor and an account of her own scientific accomplishments, Marie simply took up exactly where Pierre had left off in his last lecture.

> *"I could not forget, however, what my husband used to say, that even deprived of him, I ought to continue my work."*[29]
>
> —Marie Curie.

Marie's chief concern at this time was her continuing work on radium and radioactive elements. In August 1906 a challenge to the Curies' work had arisen from a surprising quarter. The Scottish physicist Lord Kelvin, a longtime supporter of Pierre, had published a letter in the *London Times* in which he theorized that radium was not an element at all, but merely a compound of lead and helium atoms. He went on to suggest that the Curies' Nobel Prize was a mistake. Angered by Kelvin's attack, Marie realized his influence among scientists could threaten the whole basis of her research on radioactivity. It was necessary to prove beyond a doubt that radium was a separate element with its own specific slot in the periodic table of elements. The small amounts of radium the Curies had produced up till now had been consequential but not entirely pure. Marie embarked on a new series of painstaking tests and processes that lasted several years. Aided by her colleague and lab assistant, André Debierne, she eventually was able to measure the precise atomic weight of radium—that being the average mass of its atoms—and affirm its place in the periodic table. In 1910 Marie Curie and André Debierne managed to isolate a few grains of pure radium in metallic form, another vindication of the Curies' earlier work.

The Radium Institute

Above all, Marie longed to create a permanent research facility as tribute to Pierre and the groundbreaking research they had performed together. Marie's worldwide fame and her connections in the scientific community proved very helpful to her plans. In 1907 Andrew Carnegie, the American steel magnate and philanthropist, donated $50,000

Although Curie took on teaching and lecturing duties, her first priority was always lab work. She is pictured here in her lab, surrounded by scientific equipment.

An Exceptional Education

After her husband's death, Marie Curie lavished extra attention on her daughters. She moved the family to Pierre's boyhood town, Sceaux, even though the commute to Paris required an extra hour each day. Marie was determined that the girls should enjoy the healthier atmosphere of the French countryside. She would accompany them on long walks, pointing out details in nature and encouraging questions just as her father had done with her and her siblings.

Marie had strong ideas about education. At age nine, Irène already showed signs of her lifelong interest in science. Marie doubted that French public schools could provide sufficient background in science and the arts for exceptional children. She decided to join with friends who had children of roughly the same age to organize a private school. The parents themselves, many of them prominent professors, took turns teaching. The ten or twelve students might spend one day with an expert on Chinese culture and the next take sculpting lessons from a professional artist. There were field trips to museums and concerts. Marie and the other parents avoided boring routines and tried to stimulate the children's curiosity. "Marie took the view that scientific subjects should be taught at an early age but not according to a too rigid curriculum," writes biographer Nanny Fröman. "It was important for children to be able to develop freely." In organizing this unique school, Marie no doubt drew on her own experience in Warsaw's so-called Floating Academy.

Nanny Fröman, "Marie and Pierre Curie and the Discovery of Polonium and Radium," Nobelprize.org, December 1, 1996. www.nobelprize.org.

to establish the Curie Foundation. The foundation set up a new research laboratory and paid for scholarships so that Marie could recruit promising scientists to work in the lab full time. Moreover, the French government, with its liberal zeal for scientific progress, offered more financial support. The government-funded Sorbonne joined with the private Pasteur Foundation to create the Radium Institute. This first-class facility would consist of two divisions, one for Marie's general research into radioactivity, the other for medical research. As the Radium Institute became reality, Marie could not help recalling the days when she and Pierre would process vats of pitchblende sludge in the glass-roofed shed or the open courtyard. She looked forward to many fruitful years in her new laboratory.

Marie soon became swamped with work and obligations. She reluctantly gave up her long-standing job at the women's teachers college, although she continued to support academic opportunities for females. It was hard to find time for research work between preparing and giving lectures, handling details about the Radium Institute, and caring for Irène and Ève. Yet in 1910 she managed to publish a large two-volume textbook, *A Treatise on Radioactivity*. Marie's restless and inquisitive nature kept driving her to succeed.

Chapter Five

A Living Legend

In the years after her husband's death, Marie Curie wanted nothing more than to be left alone to concentrate on research. Yet since receiving the Nobel Prize in 1903, the great Madame Curie had constantly been in the news. Her role as the world's most visible and successful female scientist, in a period when science was bringing more rapid changes to society than ever before, made her a source of constant interest and curiosity. Reporters and photographers rushed to record each new milestone, from her first lecture at the Sorbonne to her plans for the Radium Institute. Her name became synonymous in the public mind with the mysterious new phenomenon of radioactivity. This link became even more emphatic when the International Congress on Radiology and Electricity named the unit for measuring radioactivity the *curie*. (The board intended the name as a tribute to both Pierre and Marie.) Curie's growing reputation certainly helped her obtain funding for her work. But public scrutiny had its drawbacks as well. The next few years would be filled with controversy and scandal.

A Contentious Election

A dry subject such as election to the French Academy of Sciences would seem to lack any potential for controversy in the tabloid press. However, the public's interest was aroused when one of the candidates was Marie Curie. At the end of 1910, a single seat reserved for a physicist fell open at the academy. Among seven candidates, two main contenders emerged for the seat—Marie Curie and an inventor in wireless telegraphy, the sixty-six-year-old Édouard Branly, a Frenchman. The fact that Curie was even being considered was remarkable, since until recently the academy had banned females from consideration. Now the press focused breathlessly on the contest. One paper ran a photo collage featuring Curie and Branly weighed in the balance on giant scales.

Despite some trouble with overzealous reporters, Curie had grown used to favorable coverage in French newspapers. Many stories had described this brilliant, courageous woman raising her two daughters alone and working tirelessly to build the Radium Institute in honor of her dead husband. The liberal press continued to support Curie in her candidacy. The right-wing press, however, backed Branly. Angry editorials expressed a patriotic view, reminding readers that Branly had been passed over for the 1909 Nobel Prize in Physics in favor of the Italian Guglielmo Marconi. Now the honor of France demanded that he, not this émigré woman from Poland, get the seat in the French Academy of Sciences. French Catholics supported Branly on religious grounds against Curie and her freethinking friends. As passions rose on both sides, the accusations grew ridiculous. Curie's role in the discovery of radium was questioned. The right-wing daily *Excelsior* resorted to a front-page story in which it purported to conduct a scientific analysis of Curie's facial structure and handwriting. Based on this so-called analysis, the paper then erroneously concluded that she was actually Jewish and should be rejected on racial grounds. The historian Eva Hemmungs Wirtén believes the contest was like a referendum on modern society, with Curie's opponents fearful about women obtaining too much freedom:

> Indeed, many felt that what was at stake in the choice between Branly and Curie was much more than the question of whether a woman should be accepted into the Académie. The choice was between two worlds, not two sexes.... There could be little doubt that a vote for Curie was a vote for emotional turmoil and coat turning, whereas a vote for Branly meant recognizing universal values and tradition.[30]

On January 23, 1911, Branly won the seat by two votes. Conservative papers hailed this victory for justice and patriotism. Curie's reaction to the vote is not recorded. Her supporters urged her to try again, but she preferred to concentrate on her work. In her memoir, she insisted, "I do not ever wish to renew my candidacy, because of

A worker conducts testing at the Radium Institute, a research facility that Curie helped create as a tribute to Pierre and the scientific investigations the couple performed together.

my strong distaste for the personal solicitation required."[31] It was not until 1979, sixty-eight years later, that a female candidate finally won election to the French Academy of Sciences.

The Langevin Scandal

Curie was mostly relieved to put the academy episode behind her. She had plenty to occupy her thoughts at this time. She made frequent trips around Europe to accept honorary degrees and attend scientific conferences. Besides research work and caring for the children, she also found herself involved in a new relationship. And once again, due to her celebrity, the tabloids were about to descend in force.

Paul Langevin was a brilliant French physicist and one of Pierre Curie's favorite pupils. Langevin and his wife had vacationed with the

Curies, and their children often played together. After Pierre's death, Marie had appreciated Paul's consoling words and the fact that they shared so many of the same interests. They met frequently to organize the children's cooperative school and discuss research topics. As their conversations grew more intimate, Paul admitted that his marriage was unhappy. His wife, Jeanne, did not share his passion for science and complained that he was neglecting her and their four children. Soon Marie and Paul began a secret affair. Rumors spread among their friends, particularly when Paul turned down lucrative job offers to work alongside Marie. Inevitably, Paul's wife discovered the truth and filed for a legal separation.

French tabloids splashed the story across the front pages, expressing outrage that Madame Curie, the great scientist and grieving widow, should have a relationship with a married colleague. Somehow the press obtained love letters the two had exchanged and did not hesitate to print them. The letters, tame by today's standards, left little doubt about the couple's true feelings. Leery of the scandal, officials at the Sorbonne considered firing their most celebrated professor. Curie's job was saved only because her colleagues and friends at the university rallied on her behalf.

> *"I do not ever wish to renew my candidacy [for the French Academy of Sciences], because of my strong distaste for the personal solicitation required."*[31]
>
> —Marie Curie.

A Nobel Prize in Chemistry

In the midst of the Langevin controversy, Curie received some heartening news. The Stockholm committee had awarded her a second Nobel Prize, this time in chemistry. The citation declared that the award was "in recognition of her services to the advancement of chemistry by the discovery of the elements radium and polonium, by the isolation of radium and the study of the nature and compounds of this remarkable element."[32] The award was an astounding—and very welcome—endorsement of her dedicated research. It essentially honored Pierre's work, too, although posthumous awards were not given. Thus Marie Curie, already the only woman to have won the

Nobel Prize, was now the only person to have won it twice. The Paris press, still obsessed with the marital scandal, played down the award's significance.

Some members of the Royal Swedish Academy of Sciences worried that Curie's recent troubles would prove embarrassing. A letter arrived from Stockholm advising that she forego the trip to receive the award in person. Curie's response was reserved but firm. "I believe that there is no connection between my scientific work and the facts of private life," she wrote. "I cannot accept the idea in principle that the appreciation of the value of scientific work should be influenced by libel and slander concerning private life. I am convinced that this opinion is shared by many people."[33] Having missed the earlier awards ceremony due to illness, Curie was determined to attend this one. With her daughter Irène and her sister Bronya, she traveled to Stockholm and delivered to the assembled scientists and dignitaries a memorable address describing her work that led to the discovery of the new elements.

> "I cannot accept the idea in principle that the appreciation of the value of scientific work should be influenced by libel and slander concerning private life. I am convinced that this opinion is shared by many people."[33]
>
> —A letter from Marie Curie to the Nobel Committee in Stockholm, Sweden.

Again in 1911 some scientists questioned whether Marie Curie deserved this second award. In its decision, however, the Nobel committee displayed canny judgment. The Curies' 1903 prize for physics, which they shared with Antoine-Henri Becquerel, had specifically addressed the discovery of uranium rays and the Curies' crucial perception that the rays provided clues about the structure of the atom. In succeeding years other physicists, especially Ernest Rutherford, built on that perception in their studies of atomic structure. Rutherford performed tests in which he fired radioactive particles at atoms, revealing atoms to be not solid units but composed mostly of empty space, each with a core nucleus surrounded by charged electrons. By contrast, Marie Curie's 1911 prize for chemistry recognized her work in chemical analysis, probing the nature of radium and polonium. In particular, this analysis sug-

Marie Curie's 1911 Nobel Lecture

The following are excerpts from the lecture Marie Curie presented to the Royal Swedish Academy of Sciences on the occasion of her receiving the 1911 Nobel Prize in Chemistry.

Some 15 years ago the radiation of uranium was discovered by Henri Becquerel, and two years later the study of this phenomenon was extended to other substances, first by me, and then by Pierre Curie and myself. This study rapidly led us to the discovery of new elements, the radiation of which, while being analogous with that of uranium, was far more intense. All the elements emitting such radiation I have termed *radioactive*, and the new property of matter revealed in this emission has thus received the name *radioactivity*. . . .

In this field the importance of radium from the viewpoint of general theories has been decisive. The history of the discovery and the isolation of this substance has furnished proof of my hypothesis *that radioactivity is an atomic property of matter and can provide a means of seeking new elements. . . .*

Viewing the subject from this angle, it can be said that the task of isolating radium is the corner-stone of the edifice of the science of radioactivity. Moreover, radium remains the most useful and powerful tool in radioactivity laboratories. I believe that it is because of these considerations that the Swedish Academy of Sciences has done me the very great honour of awarding me this year's Nobel Prize for Chemistry.

Marie Curie, "Nobel Lecture, December 11, 1911: Radium and the New Concepts in Chemistry," Nobelprize.org, 2015. www.nobelprize.org.

gested the medical uses for radium, including the diagnosis and treatment of diseases such as cancer. Since Curie's breakthroughs occurred in two different disciplines, science historians believe her two Nobel Prizes were fully justified.

After her triumphant appearance in Sweden, Curie returned home exhausted and ill. Months of turmoil had left her plagued by depression and a painful kidney ailment. In January 1912 she entered a private clinic under a false name and eventually underwent kidney surgery. The procedure was a success, but afterward Curie suffered a complete nervous collapse. She withdrew to a secret address near Paris, where she used her maiden name, Sklodowska, to avoid press inquiries. It was almost a full year before she was able to return to the lab. During her period of seclusion, Curie did receive a visit from a delegation of Polish intellectuals. The group appealed to her patriotic feelings, urging her to abandon the scandal-obsessed Parisians and relocate her Radium Institute to Poland. Touched by this plea, Curie nevertheless had to decline. As a tribute to her husband's memory, she believed the Radium Institute belonged in France, and she intended to honor her original commitment. She did, however, direct two of her gifted Polish assistants to help establish a similar institute in Warsaw.

Service During the War

The Radium Institute finally opened its doors in Paris in August 1914, soon after World War I broke out in Europe. As German battalions invaded Belgium and northeastern France, the French government evacuated Paris for the city of Bordeaux in the southwest. With German troops likely to attack Paris, work at the institute was out of the question. Curie arranged for her daughters to stay in Brittany on the coast, where they had spent the summer with friends. At the government's urging, she left for Bordeaux, carrying with her on the train a lead-lined box. Inside was a single gram of pure radium, the entire supply that existed in all of France. Curie was determined to secure the precious element for her research. Once the radium was hidden in Bordeaux, safe from enemy hands, she returned to Paris.

With Germany threatening her beloved Poland as well as her adopted country of France, Curie was determined to serve the Allied cause. She decided to devote her efforts to saving lives by way of a familiar technology: X-rays. Enlisting the help of the Red Cross, she was able to equip a fleet of twenty trucks with X-ray equipment powered by the engine batteries. The trucks, which grateful soldiers began to call *les Petites Curie* (Little Curies), could transport bulky X-ray machines to battlefield hospitals. There doctors used the machines to pinpoint bullet and shrapnel wounds and examine broken bones for immediate surgery. Curie herself learned to drive one of the vans and operate the X-ray equipment. Seventeen-year-old Irène, with a quick mind and an appetite for new experiences, joined Marie as her first assistant. Having spent too much time apart from her mother in the last few years, Irène treasured their shared adventure in the mobile X-ray unit.

Campaigning for Radium

In 1916 Paris seemed safe from German threat, and Marie Curie returned to work at the Radium Institute. Retrieving the gram of radium from Bordeaux, she used it to collect radon, a radioactive gas, in very thin glass tubes. Doctors could inject one of these tubes into a patient's body at the precise spot to attack diseased tissue—a technique that looked forward to modern radiation therapy. Curie also trained women to assist in radiology exams. Her war experience with X-ray machines had reaffirmed the usefulness of radiation technology.

After the war, Curie worked tirelessly to promote the Radium Institute. Her innate shyness would disappear when she had to approach rich business owners or philanthropists for donations or other assistance. Due to Curie's long-standing links with French industry, the Radium Institute was able to maintain its stock of the precious element for which it was named. Nonetheless, Curie dreamed of doubling that single gram of radium in order to expand her research. In May 1920 she explained to Marie Mattingly Meloney, a visiting American journalist, that the United States had fifty times more radium than her world-renowned laboratory. The interview, appearing in a popular American magazine for women, led to the Marie Curie Radium Campaign. It was an organized drive to fund the great woman scientist's life work. Marie also wrote a brief autobiography for publication in America. The amazing story of Madame Curie's heroic rise in the male-dominated world of science appealed to the can-do spirit of Americans and led to a flood of public support and donations.

On a 1921 trip to the United States, Curie met dignitaries, including President Warren G. Harding, with whom she is pictured here.

In 1921, to cap the successful campaign, Curie and her daughters sailed to the United States. During her whirlwind tour Curie spoke to delighted audiences and met scientists, business leaders, celebrities, and politicians, including President Warren G. Harding at a White House reception. She shook so many hands in the first days of the tour that she finally placed her right arm in a sling to discourage well-wishers. By tour's end she had amassed equipment, ore samples, cash donations for the institute, and a second gram of precious radium. This remarkable woman—frail, shy, prematurely aged, dressed in black, and speaking softly with a Polish accent—had become for millions a living legend.

Madame Curie's Final Years and Legacy

Curie's triumphant trip to America helped restore her reputation. Some of this was due to exaggerated claims for radium therapy. "Curie Cures Cancer! In May of 1921, this headline appeared in newspapers across America," writes biographer Barbara Goldsmith. "This claim alleviated a fear of death and struck a deep chord in America's collective psyche."[34] Curie was not responsible for such

Irène Curie and Frédéric Joliot

From a young age it was obvious that Irène Curie shared with her famous parents the same penetrating intellect. Growing up, Irène and her sister, Ève, often did not see Marie for days or weeks at a time. Yet Irène dreamed of following her mother's path and one day making her own lasting contribution to science. For her doctorate Irène focused on the study of polonium, one of the elements her mother had discovered. Working in the laboratory with Marie, Irène grew fond of another lab assistant, Frédéric Joliot. Like Irène's parents, she and Frédéric came to depend on each other professionally and personally. Because young Frédéric lacked Irène's academic credentials, some observers thought he was using Irène to advance his career. In fact, Marie herself had doubts, but the couple's marriage proved strong.

In the 1930s the Joliot-Curies pursued their own research on radiation and atomic structure. Like physicists around the world, they furiously sought to identify and describe new atomic particles. They narrowly missed being first to discover the neutron and the positron. Like her mother, Irène suffered from radiation sickness, and she also developed tuberculosis, a deadly lung disease. Nevertheless, she refused to slow the pace of her work. In January 1934 Frédéric bombarded aluminum with alpha particles, producing a so-called radioisotope—a radioactive cousin of phosphorus. He and Irène had discovered artificial radioactivity, for which they won their own Nobel Prize. Irène's mother, with only months to live, was able to witness her daughter's triumph.

Irène Curie, Marie's elder daughter, followed in her mother's scientific footsteps, winning the 1935 Nobel Prize in Chemistry alongside her husband, Frédéric. The couple is pictured here.

claims, but she saw how they could boost fund-raising and did little to discourage them. The French establishment also opened its arms to the venerable scientist. The previously all-male Académie Nationale de Médecine (National Academy of Medicine) in Paris welcomed her as a member largely because of her research into radium therapy.

Years of working with radioactive materials took their toll on Curie's health. In the early 1930s she often felt too weak to go to the lab. She finally sought treatment in Geneva, Switzerland, where doctors diagnosed aplastic pernicious anemia, a disease of the bone marrow. Experts today believe Curie's unprotected work with X-ray machines during the war may have been more harmful than her radium exposure. On July 4, 1934, she died. Tributes poured in from around the world as Marie Curie was laid to rest in the Sceaux cemetery next to her beloved Pierre.

Curie's rich legacy in science is twofold—as an innovative researcher in her own right and as an inspiration to women in science everywhere. Her discovery, with Pierre, of the radioactive elements radium and polonium contributed to new insights about the nature of radiation and the structure of atoms. Through Marie's efforts, the Radium Institute became one of the world's top facilities for research into radioactivity and medical uses for radiation. Her study of radioactivity is in many ways the starting point for the atomic age, which would encompass nuclear energy, the atomic bomb, cancer treatment, radiocarbon dating, and even molecular biology and modern genetics. Her additional role, as an inspirational example for other female scientists, began at home. Her brilliant daughter Irène also became a physicist, marrying another scientist at the institute, Frédéric Joliot, in 1926. The couple won the Nobel Prize in Chemistry in 1935, the third such award in the Curie family. But it is the story of Marie Curie's persistent quest to make her mark in science that has inspired so many women in the field. "Madame Curie was the mother of us all," explains science writer Natalie Angier, "a role model for every girl who stakes a claim to a life of the mind, particularly that part of the mind too often deemed masculine—the scientific, mathematical part. I have interviewed hundreds of female scientists over the years, and a number of them have told me how, in their girlhood, the story of Madame Curie captivated and inspired them."[35]

> *"Madame Curie was the mother of us all, a role model for every girl who stakes a claim to a life of the mind, particularly that part of the mind too often deemed masculine—the scientific, mathematical part."*[35]
>
> —Science writer Natalie Angier.

Source Notes

Introduction: A Hazardous Collection

1. Quoted in Adam Clark Estes, "Marie Curie's Century-Old Radioactive Notebook Still Requires Lead Box," *Factually* (blog), August 4, 2014. http://factually.gizmodo.com.

2. Quoted in Ivy F. Kupec, "Diversity in Science," National Science Foundation, November 7, 2013. www.nsf.gov.

Chapter 1: The Floating University

3. Marie Curie, *Pierre Curie: With Autobiographical Notes by Marie Curie*. New York: Dover, 2012, p. 79.

4. Ève Curie, *Madame Curie*. New York: Da Capo, 2001, p. 6.

5. Quoted in Curie, *Madame Curie*, p. 43.

6. Megan Abigail White, "Poland's Flying Universities," *History Blog*, May 31, 2010. http://meganabigail.blogspot.com.

7. Quoted in Susan Quinn, *Marie Curie: A Life*. Lexington, MA: Plunkett Lake, 2011, p. 67.

8. Quoted in Quinn, *Marie Curie*, p. 79.

Chapter 2: An Education in Paris

9. Quoted in Sarah Dry and Sabine Seifert, *Curie*. London: Haus, 2003, p. 14.

10. Quoted in Quinn, *Marie Curie*, p. 89.

11. Quoted in American Institute of Physics, "A Poor Student in Paris." www.aip.org.

12. Quoted in Craig Nelson, *The Age of Radiance: The Epic Rise and Dramatic Fall of the Atomic Era*. New York: Scribner, 2014, p. 23.

13. Quoted in *APS News*, "March 1880: The Curie Brothers Discover Piezoelectricity," March 2014. www.aps.org.

14. Quoted in Mark Trombetta, "Madame Maria Sklodowska-Curie—Brilliant Scientist, Humanitarian, Humble Hero: Poland's Gift to the World," *Journal of Contemporary Brachytherapy*, September 10, 2014. www.ncbi.nlm.nih.gov.

15. Quoted in Alan E. Waltar, *Radiation and Modern Life: Fulfilling Marie Curie's Dream*. New York: Prometheus, 2004, p. 15.

Chapter 3: Discovering Radium

16. Hannah Waters, "The First X-Ray, 1895," *Scientist*, July 1, 2011. www.the-scientist.com.

17. Carolyn Gramling, "Benchmarks: Becquerel Discovers Radioactivity on February 26, 1896," *Earth: The Science Behind the Headlines*, February 28, 2011. www.earthmagazine.org.

18. Marie Curie, "The Dream Becomes a Reality: The Discovery of Radium," *Lateral Science* (blog), July 8, 2012. http://lateralscience.blogspot.com.

19. Denise Ham, "Marie Sklodowska Curie: The Woman Who Opened the Nuclear Age," *21st Century*, Winter 2002–2003. www.21stcenturysciencetech.com.

20. Curie, "The Dream Becomes a Reality."

21. Curie, "The Dream Becomes a Reality."

22. Quoted in Ham, "Marie Sklodowska Curie."

23. Quoted in American Institute of Physics, "Marie Curie in Her Own Words: The Struggle to Isolate Radium." www.aip.org.

Chapter 4: A Tragic Death

24. Quoted in American Institute of Physics, "Marie Curie and the Science of Radioactivity: Honors from Abroad." www.aip.org.

25. Nanny Fröman, "Marie and Pierre Curie and the Discovery of Polonium and Radium," Nobelprize.org, December 1, 1996. www.nobelprize.org.

26. Quoted in Don Lincoln, *Understanding the Universe: From Quarks to the Cosmos*. New Jersey: World Scientific, 2012, p. 36.

27. Quoted in Diana Preston, *Before the Fallout: From Marie Curie to Hiroshima*. New York: Bloomsbury, 2009, p. 119.

28. Quoted in Quinn, *Marie Curie*, p. 237.

29. Quoted in Sheri Stritof, "Fellow Scientists Marie and Pierre Curie Had a Remarkable Marriage," About.com: About Relationships, 2015. http://marriage.about.com.

Chapter 5: A Living Legend

30. Eva Hemmungs Wirtén, *Making Marie Curie: Intellectual Property and Celebrity Culture in an Age of Information*. Chicago: University of Chicago Press, 2015, p. 53.

31. Curie, *Pierre Curie*, p. 99.

32. Nobel Foundation, "The Nobel Prize in Chemistry 1911," Nobelprize.org, 2015. www.nobelprize.org.

33. Quoted in Barbara Goldsmith, *Obsessive Genius: The Inner World of Marie Curie*. New York: Norton, 2005, p. 178.

34. Goldsmith, *Obsessive Genius*, p. 191.

35. Natalie Angier, introduction to *Madame Curie: A Biography*, by Ève Curie. New York: Da Capo, 2001, p. xi.

Important Events in the Life of Marie Curie

1867

Marie Sklodowska is born May 15 in Warsaw, Poland.

1884

Marie begins to attend the Floating University, an illegal night school.

1886

Marie starts working as a governess to support her sister Bronya's university studies in Paris, France.

1891

Marie travels to Paris to begin taking classes at the Sorbonne.

1893

Marie earns her undergraduate degree in physics, the first woman to do so at the Sorbonne.

1894

While seeking lab facilities for a job, Marie meets a scientist and teacher named Pierre Curie.

1895

Marie marries Pierre Curie in a Paris suburb.

1896

Marie reads about Antoine-Henri Becquerel's discovery of uranium rays and decides to study them for her doctorate.

1898

Marie discovers polonium on February 17 and, with Pierre, discovers radium on December 26.

1903

Marie and Pierre, along with Becquerel, are awarded the Nobel Prize in Physics.

1906

Pierre is struck by a horse-drawn wagon on a Paris street and dies instantly.

1911

Marie is awarded the Nobel Prize in Chemistry.

1914

The Radium Institute, dedicated to Pierre's memory, opens in Paris.

1915

Marie and her daughter Irène lead a fleet of X-ray trucks to treat battlefield injuries during World War I.

1921

Marie tours the United States to raise funds for the Radium Institute.

1929

Marie makes her final fund-raising trip to the United States.

1934

Marie Curie dies on July 4 of aplastic pernicious anemia, likely due to radiation exposure.

1935

Marie's daughter Irène and her husband, Frédéric Joliot, win the Nobel Prize in Chemistry.

For Further Research

Books

Wayne Biddle, *A Field Guide to Radiation*. New York: Penguin, 2012.

Ève Curie, *Madame Curie*. New York: Da Capo, 2001.

Craig Nelson, *The Age of Radiance: The Epic Rise and Dramatic Fall of the Atomic Era*. New York: Scribner, 2014.

Diana Preston, *Before the Fallout: From Marie Curie to Hiroshima*. New York: Bloomsbury, 2009.

Susan Quinn, *Marie Curie: A Life*. Lexington, MA: Plunkett Lake, 2011.

Eva Hemmungs Wirtén, *Making Marie Curie: Intellectual Property and Celebrity Culture in an Age of Information*. Chicago: University of Chicago Press, 2015.

Internet Sources

Julie Des Jardins, "Madame Curie's Passion," *Smithsonian*, October 2011. www.smithsonianmag.com/history/madame-curies-passion-74 183598/?no-ist.

Adam Clark Estes, "Marie Curie's Century-Old Radioactive Notebook Still Requires Lead Box," *Factually* (blog), August 4, 2014. http://factually.gizmodo.com/marie-curies-100-year-old-notebook -is-still-too-radioac-1615847891.

Nanny Fröman, "Marie and Pierre Curie and the Discovery of Polonium and Radium," Nobelprize.org, December 1, 1996. www.nobel prize.org/nobel_prizes/themes/physics/curie.

Denise Ham, "Marie Sklodowska Curie: The Woman Who Opened the Nuclear Age," *21st Century*, Winter 2002–2003. www .21stcenturysciencetech.com/articles/wint02-03/Marie_Curie.pdf.

Sheri Stritof, "Fellow Scientists Marie and Pierre Curie Had a Remarkable Marriage," About.com: About Relationships, 2015. http://marriage.about.com/od/historical/fl/Fellow-Scientists-Marie-and-Pierre-Curie-Had-a-Remarkable-Marriage.htm.

Websites

Discovery of Radioactivity (www.vigyanprasar.gov.in/dream/apr 2001/RADIOACTIVITY.htm). This website presents an overview of research into radioactivity, including scientists from Becquerel and the Curies to Rutherford.

Maria Sklodowska-Curie (www.staff.amu.edu.pl/~zbzw/ph/sci/msc .htm). This website includes a biography of Marie Curie as well as many entertaining features and interesting facts connected to her life and achievement.

Marie Curie and the Science of Radioactivity (www.aip.org/history /curie/contents.htm). This website created by the American Institute of Physics provides a detailed and colorful biography of Marie Curie and also includes background articles on related topics.

Nobelprize.org (www.nobelprize.org). This website contains the full texts of Pierre Curie's lecture for the 1903 Nobel Prize and Marie Curie's lecture for the 1911 Nobel Prize. These lectures explain the importance of the discoveries that led to the awards.

Index

Picture Credits